To ....

HAPPY HALLOWEEN!

Love, ...

....

TRICK OR TREAT IN PENNSYLVANIA

Written by Eric James

Illustrated by Karl West

A HALLOWEEN ADVENTURE IN THE KEYSTONE STATE

sourcebooks
jabberwocky

The full moon's out on Halloween.
The sky is starry bright.
Above the state of Pennsylvania
appears an eerie light.

It darts behind the scattered clouds.
It zips from town to town.
It hovers over Allentown,
then slowly heads on down.

POCONO MOUNTAINS

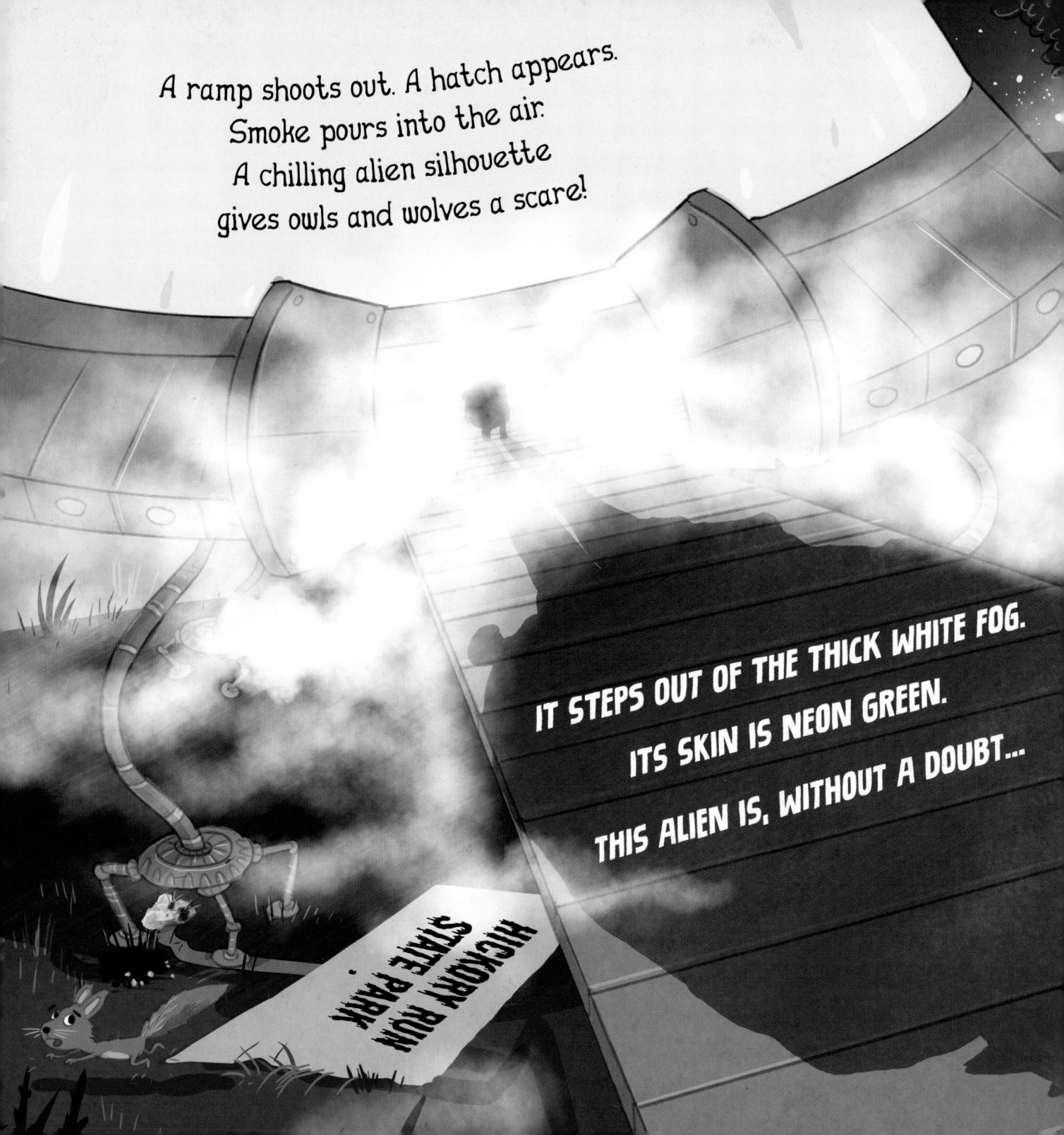

A ramp shoots out. A hatch appears.
Smoke pours into the air.
A chilling alien silhouette
gives owls and wolves a scare!

IT STEPS OUT OF THE THICK WHITE FOG.

ITS SKIN IS NEON GREEN.

THIS ALIEN IS, WITHOUT A DOUBT...

HICKORY RUN
STATE PARK

...the cutest thing I've seen!

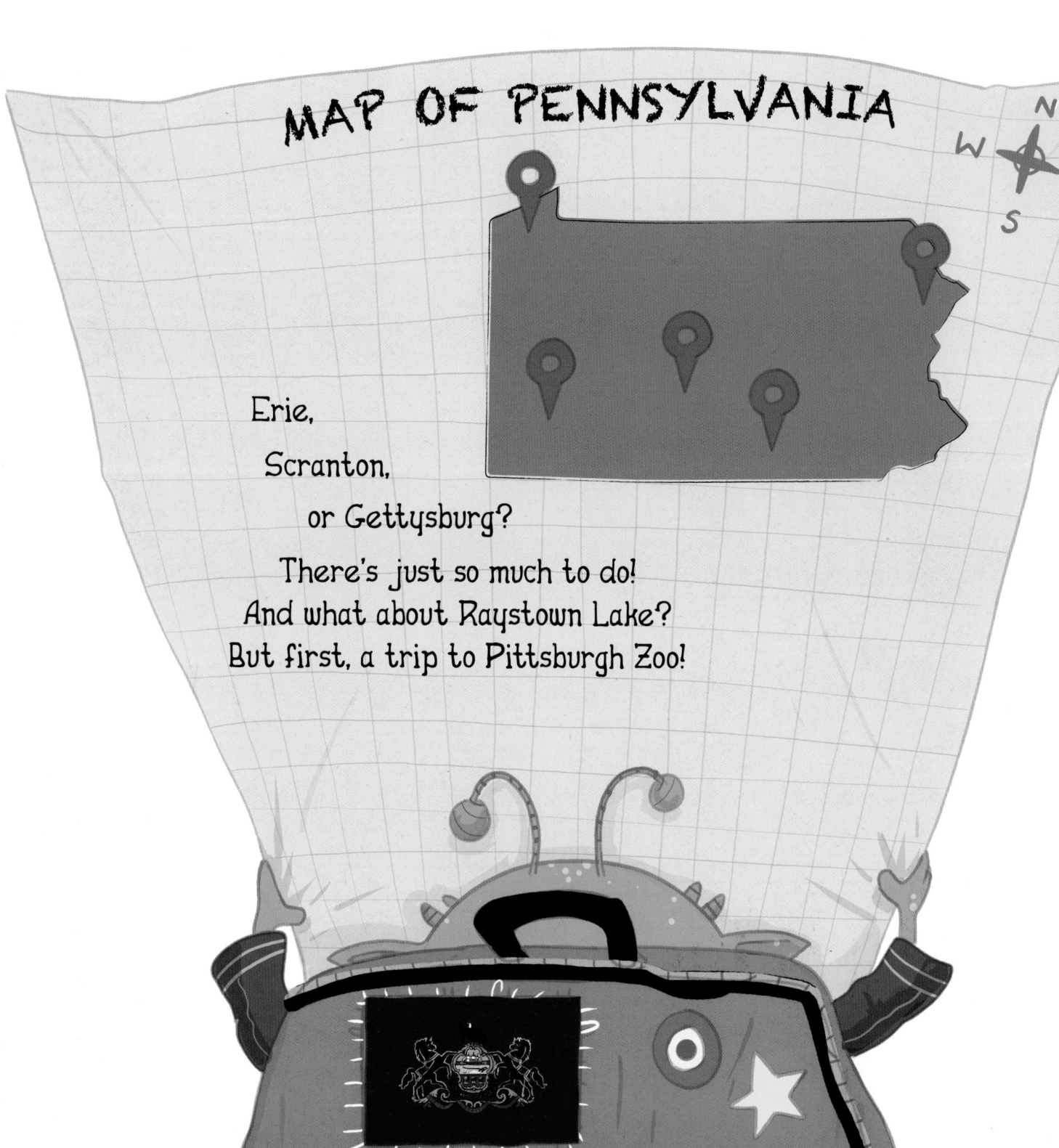

MAP OF PENNSYLVANIA

Erie,

Scranton,

or Gettysburg?

There's just so much to do!
And what about Raystown Lake?
But first, a trip to Pittsburgh Zoo!

He pulls out his transporter,

and waves it in the air.

Now in the spot where he just stood there is...nobody there!

He reappears in Pittsburgh,
and wanders all around,
making sure that he checks off
each landmark that he's found.

TOP 5 TOURIST SPOTS

1 PITTSBURGH ZOO & PPG AQUARIUM

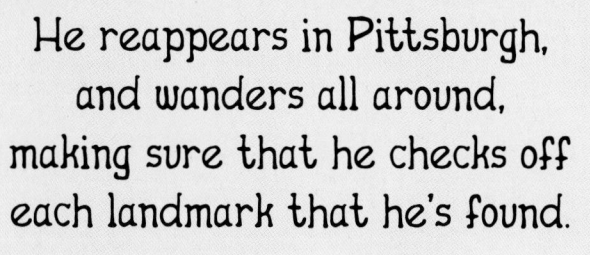

2 STATE CAPITOL, HARRISBURG

3 HERSHEYPARK, HERSHEY

4 KNOEBELS AMUSEMENT RESORT, ELYSBURG

5 GETTYSBURG NATIONAL MILITARY PARK

I ♥ PENNSYLVANIA

He zaps to Philadelphia
to take a little look.
Snapping selfies as he goes,

and posting them to **Spacebook.**

But where is everybody?
Are they staying in tonight?
He climbs up high to take a peek
and gets a nasty fright.

For all around this spooky town,
the streets are jammed and heaving.

MONSTERS, MONSTERS EVERYWHERE!

It's time that he was leaving!

EASTERN
HEMLOCK
PARK

"I'd better run," the alien says.
"I'm not a big brave hero!
Oh no! My gizmo doesn't work!
The battery gauge reads ZERO."

They're closing in. There's no escape!
He scrunches up his eyes.
The monsters all surround him, but...
he gets a big surprise!

"Hey, high five, dude!" a vampire shouts.
"Great costume," shrieks a ghoul.
A little ghost tugs at his arm
and says, "I think you're cool."

"So you don't want to eat me then?"
the little alien asks.
They laugh until they're so red-faced
they must take off their masks.

"Sweet antennae," smiles the ghost,
while giving them a flick.
The children shriek—what happens next
is just the coolest trick...

The jack-o'-lanterns all take off

and

float

into the sky!

"Oh, wow!" they gasp. "It looks like you're
a real-life alien guy!"

The children dance excitedly.
They shout, "Can you do more?"

The alien shows them lots of tricks
as they go door to door.

These antics impress everyone,
which comes in really handy,

because it means before too long
their bags are FILLED with candy!

"It's getting late. I'd better go,"
the alien says at last.
"I promise I'll come back next year.

PENNSYLVANIA'S A BLAST!"

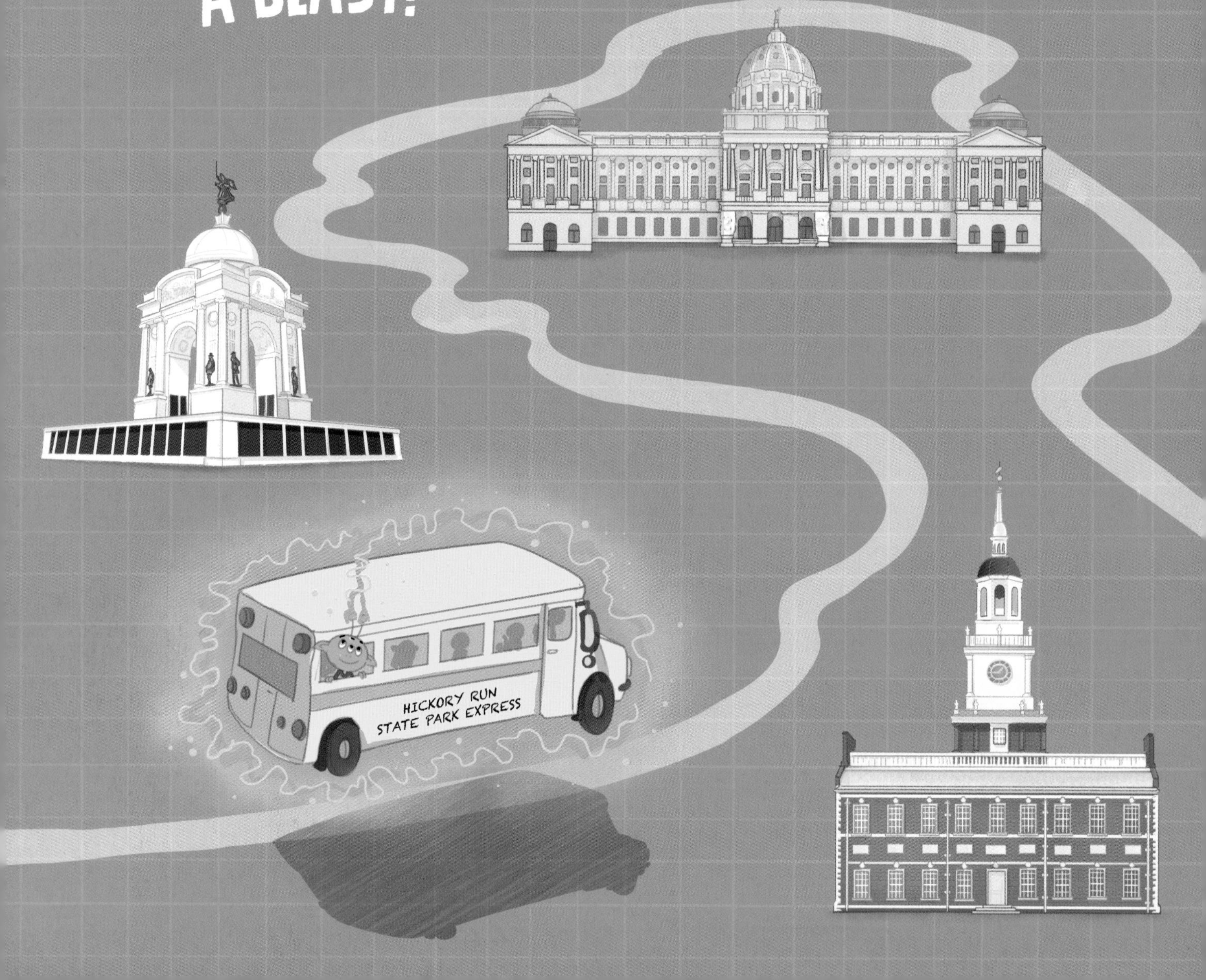

They take him to his spaceship,
and say their sad goodbyes.
They wait for him to start it up,
and zoom into the skies.

HICKORY RUN
STATE PARK

HERSHEYPARK

I ♥ PENNSYLVANIA

His spaceship has a fuel leak—
there's thick goo everywhere.
"Aw shucks," he says, "it looks like
I'm not going anywhere!"

I ♥ PENNSYLVANIA

"We'll fill the tank with candy.
We've got buckets of the stuff!
Throw it in, up to the brim.
That should be just enough."

The spaceship is now ready.
The alien turns the key.
The engine roars, the spaceship soars,
and zooms off with a...

WHEEEEEEEEEEEEEEEEEE

But now it's diving back to Earth;
the children shake with fear.
Aaah! He's just flying past to wave
and say, "See you next year!"

Written by Eric James
Illustrated by Karl West
Additional artwork by Srimalie Bassani
Designed by Ryan Dunn

Published by Sourcebooks Jabberwocky,
an imprint of Sourcebooks, Inc.
P.O. Box 4410, Naperville, Illinois 60567-4410
(630) 961-3900
jabberwockykids.com

Date of Production: May 2019
Run Number: 5013978
Printed and bound in China (WKT)
10 9 8 7 6 5 4 3 2 1